ABOUT THE BANK STREET READY-TO-READ SERIES

Seventy-five years of educational research and innovative teaching have given the Bank Street College of Education the reputation as America's most trusted name in early childhood education.

Because no two children are exactly alike in their development, we have designed the *Bank Street Ready-to-Read* series in three levels to accommodate the individual stages of reading readiness of children ages four through eight.

○ *Level 1:* GETTING READY TO READ—read-alouds for children who are taking their first steps toward reading.

● *Level 2:* READING TOGETHER—for children who are just beginning to read by themselves but may need a little help.

○ *Level 3:* I CAN READ IT MYSELF—for children who can read independently.

Our three levels make it easy to select the books most appropriate for a child's development and enable him or her to grow with the series step by step. The *Bank Street Ready-to-Read* books also overlap and reinforce each other, further encouraging the reading process.

We feel that making reading fun and enjoyable is the single most important thing that you can do to help children become good readers. And we hope you'll be a part of Bank Street's long tradition of learning through sharing.

The Bank Street College of Education

Once upon a time,
and a long time ago,
there lived a woman with two daughters.

5

Claire, the younger,
was as beautiful as she was good.
Her eyes were warm as sunshine,
    her voice was full of bells,
    and her heart was good as gold.

Malina, the older,
was ugly and mean like her mother.
Her mouth was bitter,
her face was hard,
and her heart was rusty
as old nails.

Malina and her mother hated Claire.
They made her work all the time.
She had to scrub their stockings
and press their petticoats.
They made her sit alone in the kitchen,
with nothing to eat but
the scraps from their plates.

Every morning and evening,
Claire had to fetch water from the well.
She had a long climb up a steep, rocky hill.
The heavy buckets hurt her hands,
but she took each step with a happy heart
and a merry will.

One morning, a ragged old woman
hobbled up to the well
and asked Claire for a drink.
Now, truth be told,
this old woman was really a fairy.
She had made herself look old and poor
to see if Claire's heart was
as kind as her face.

"Let me help you,"
Claire told the old woman.
She drew the clearest water
from the coolest part of the well.

She gave it to the ragged woman
with a smile and a curtsy
that made Claire's old tin cup
seem fine as silver.

"Thank you, my dear,"
the old woman said,
and she drank deeply.
"You are as polite as you are pretty.
And here is my gift for thanks.
Each time you speak,
flowers and jewels shall fall
from your mouth."

Then she disappeared before
Claire could even thank her.
Claire ran home with her heavy buckets,
laughing as water and jewels
splashed and sparkled
all around her in the sun.

"You're late!" her mother scolded
as soon as she got home.
"I'm sorry, Mother," Claire said gently.
"Let me tell you what happened."
Two roses, three diamonds,
four pearls, and a ruby
fell from her lips as she spoke.

"Dear daughter! What can this mean?"
her wicked mother asked,
suddenly acting sweet as sugar.
Jewels and flowers scattered on the floor
as Claire told her story.
The mother fell to her knees
and shoved the jewels in her pockets.

Then she yelled at Malina.
"Go to the well at once," she ordered.
"And if you meet a ragged old woman,
be sure to give her some water."
"Why should I?" the rude girl asked.

"Just look what your sister got,"
the greedy woman answered.
"Diamonds and rubies!
Emeralds and pearls!
Now do as I say!"

Malina fussed and snapped.
She whined and whimpered.
But she finally set off for the well,
dragging her feet
and carrying their best silver pitcher.
She climbed the rocky hill,
complaining every step of the way.

When Malina finally reached the well,
she met a lady dressed like a princess.

"May I please have a drink?"
the fine lady said.
Malina was so hot and thirsty
she did not even answer.

She dipped her pitcher into the well
and took a long drink of cool water.
"Please help me," the lady cried.
"I am so very thirsty."
"If you want a drink, get it yourself,"
Malina told the lady crossly.
"I am not your servant."

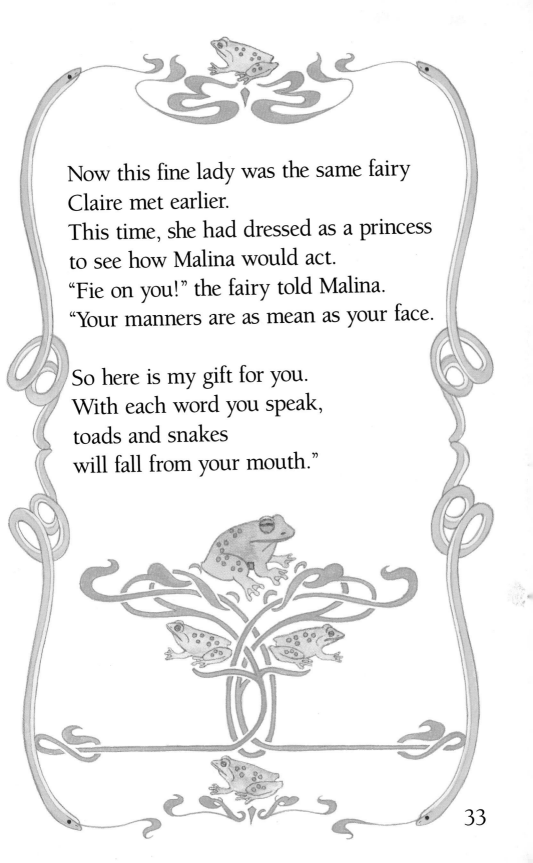

Now this fine lady was the same fairy
Claire met earlier.
This time, she had dressed as a princess
to see how Malina would act.
"Fie on you!" the fairy told Malina.
"Your manners are as mean as your face.

So here is my gift for you.
With each word you speak,
toads and snakes
will fall from your mouth."

Malina screamed and ran home,
snakes and toads tumbling from her lips.
"Mama, Mama!" she called.
"Just look what happened!"
Her mother watched with horror
as toads and snakes came pouring
from Malina's mouth.

"It's all Claire's fault," Malina shrieked
as toads hopped on her shoulders
and snakes dripped from her hair.
"You made this happen,"
the mother scolded,
and she slapped Claire.
Two tears as bright as diamonds
slid down Claire's cheeks.

Then Claire ran away,
deep into the forest,
where the sun glittered on the leaves
and the birds sang like flutes.
She ran as far and as fast as she could,
knowing she would never go home again.
Soon, she heard the drum of hoof beats.

It was the king's son,
following the trail of flowers
that sprang up each time Claire took a step.

"Why are you crying?"
the Prince asked kindly.
Claire told him her story.
By the time she was done,
the Prince was in love
with her kind heart and gentle ways.
He hardly even saw the heaps of jewels
sparkling at their feet.

"And now the whole world lies before me,"
said Claire; "I will never go home again."
"I would be honored to welcome you
to my home," said the Prince.

They filled their hands with flowers
then set off for his castle.
Everyone in the kingdom came out
to welcome them.

Claire and the Prince decided
to marry that very day.
The fairy was the very first
to give them her blessing.

When the wicked mother heard all this,
she grew sick with envy.
Malina grew meaner than ever.
She shrieked and raved.
She hissed and howled
till every room in the house
swarmed with snakes and toads.

Even her mother grew sick of her.
At last, she chased Malina into
a dark corner of the forest,
where they both lived in great misery
till they died of rage.

Claire and the Prince lived a long life
blessed with joy and plenty.
And they always remembered
the fairy's blessing:

Of all great riches
to have and hold,
a kind heart is far
more precious than gold.